101

Good Night

Stories

Reprinted in 2016 by

An imprint of Om **Books International**

Corporate & Editorial Office
A-12, Sector 64, Noida - 201 301
Uttar Pradesh, India
Phone: +91-120-477 4100
Email: editorial@ombooks.com
Website: www.ombooksinternational.com

Sales Office
107, Ansari Road, Darya Ganj
New Delhi 110 002, India
Phone: +91 11 4000 9000
Fax: +91 11 2327 8091
Email: sales@ombooks.com
Website: www.ombooks.com

ISBN 978-93-80069-59-3

Printed in India

10 9 8 7 6 5 4 3

101
Good Night
Stories

An imprint of Om Books International

Content

1 The Giant and the Miser

Once, there lived a kind-hearted giant and a miser blacksmith in the same town. The giant felt sad to know of the blacksmith's unjust treatment of his workers. "I must teach him a lesson," he thought and came up with a plan. "I will go and work under him and when he treats me badly I will show him how it hurts." So, the next morning the giant went to the blacksmith to seek work. "How much money do I need to pay you?" asked the blacksmith. "Give me whatever you can for each blow of the hammer," said the giant. The blacksmith was overjoyed at the thought that by paying only a meagre amount, he could get all his work done by the giant. Once the deal was settled, the giant took the hammer and gave such a blow that the anvil broke into pieces. The blacksmith grew worried and decided to do away with the giant. "I cannot keep you," he rumbled. "I will pay you nothing for that blow of the hammer. You leave from here, right now." "But you promised you will give me something for each blow of the hammer," reminded the giant, gently. "Ask for anything else but money," said the blacksmith grumpily. "And do not ask for too much. I won't give it," he threatened. "Just this," said the giant and kicked the blacksmith hard, sending him flying over the rooftop. "I hope you've learnt your lesson now, you miser! Don't you dare treat your workers unfairly again."

2 Little Mermaid

Long, long ago, in the Deep Sea kingdom, there lived a sea king with his five mermaid daughters. Sirenetta was the youngest and the loveliest among them. Everybody praised her voice and her beauty. One day, while swimming on the surface of the water and watching ships sail by, Sirenetta saw a young man drowning in the water. She swam swiftly to save him and dragged him to the shore where people found him while she swam away. This man was a prince. When he became conscious, he looked around for the girl who had saved him but no one knew who she was. Sirenetta had fallen in love with the prince but was disheartened as she could never become human like the prince. He had two feet and she had a fish tail! Now in the Deep Sea lived a witch with magical powers. One day, Sirenetta went to beg her for human legs. The witch said, "Sacrifice your beautiful voice! Only then shall I give you human legs! But remember, every time you set your feet on the ground, it will hurt horribly!" Sirenetta agreed, not minding the pain as all she wanted was to be with the prince. As soon as she got her two feet, she became dumb. The witch added, "If your prince marries anybody else, you shall dissolve in the sea

water and can never become a mermaid again!" With the witch's magic spell, Sirenetta found herself lying on the beach with the prince looking at her. He asked, "Where are you from?" But she could not reply. The prince took her to his palace and looked after her. They became good friends and had a wonderful time together. Every step Sirenetta took hurt, but she bore it all silently. She loved the prince but he was unaware that the beautiful maiden who had saved him and who he was in love with was right before him. Sirenetta could not tell him the truth and he could not realise it. Some time later, the prince obeyed his father's wish and went to see a neighbouring king's daughter and was enchanted by her beauty. Convinced that she was his saviour, he proposed to her. A grand wedding took place. Heartbroken, Sirenetta ran to the seashore crying and found four mermaids, her sisters! One of them handed her a knife and said, "Here, Sirenetta! This is a magic knife! We gave locks of our long hair to the witch of the Deep Sea for it. Kill your prince and you shall turn into a mermaid again!" Sirenetta took the magic knife and went to the prince's room at night. But she loved him so much that she could not kill him. She knew that, at dawn, she would vanish into the sea, just as the witch of the Deep Sea had told her. She sat on the shore and wept silently. Suddenly, there appeared a pink cloud before her, lifting her into the sky. "Where am I?" asked Sirenetta, for now she could talk. The beautiful fairies replied, "We are the air fairies. You are now one of us because you did such a good deed for the person you love." From then on, the little mermaid lived happily in the sky with the fairies.

3 Ali Baba and the Forty Thieves

Once, Ali Baba, a poor woodcutter went to the forest to chop some wood. Suddenly he saw forty thieves stopin front of a cave. The leader said, "Open Sesame!" and the sealed mouth of the cave opened magically. To close the entrance, the leader said, "Close Sesame!" and the cave sealed itself once more. Trembling with excitement, Ali Baba waited till the thieves had left and then entered the cave after saying the magic words. To his astonishment, he found piles of treasure. Ali Baba told his brother Kasim about the wondrous cave and he too set off to get some treasure for himself. Sadly, he forgot the words to leave the cave and the thieves killed him. Ali Baba discovered his brother's body in the cave and took it back to bury it with the help of Morgiana, a servant girl. Realising that someone else knew about their cave, the thieves tracked down Ali Baba. The leader, disguised as an oil seller brought along mules loaded with forty oil jars containing the other thieves.

Clever Morgiana knew who the oil seller really was and poured boiling oil into the jars, killing the thieves. While dancing before the leader to charm him, Morgiana cleverly stabbed him. Ali Baba was saved and they lived happily ever after.

4 Sindbad's Great Escape

Sindbad was a merchant's son who would travel to many a distant land trading goods. During one of his voyages, the merchant ship stopped at a beautiful island where Sindbad decided to take a nap. When he woke up, he discovered that the ship had set sail without him! As he was looking for a way to get off the island, he saw a large white dome. Just then, a huge shadow fell over him. Looking up, Sindbad saw a huge bird called the Roc and realised that the white dome was actually the bird's egg. A brilliant idea came to him. "Let me tie myself to this bird's legs!" he thought. "Then, I can leave this island." At daybreak, when the Roc flew away over the sea, it carried Sindbad too. When it landed, Sindbad untied himself quickly before the Roc flew off again. He found himself in a valley full of diamonds, surrounded by steep mountains. Large serpents roamed there day and night, making human survival there very difficult. "Thud! Thud!" Sindbad saw big chunks of meat landing on the valley floor being thrown down the ridges by merchants who wanted the diamonds. They waited for the eagles to pick up the chunks of meat with the diamonds stuck on them, and take them to their nests from where the merchants would get the diamonds. Sindbad tied himself to a piece of meat. An eagle picked him up and carried him to his nest from where he ran away as fast as he could, finding his freedom at last.

5 Androcles and the Lion

Androcles was a Roman slave who escaped from his cruel master and started living in the jungles. There, he saw an injured lion with a thorn stuck in his paw. Kind Androcles plucked out the thorn helping rid the lion of his pain. They lived together until the emperor's men recaptured Androcles. As a punishment for absconding, Androcles was thrown inside a ring to be eaten up by the lions. Lots of people, including the emperor, gathered to watch this scene. The lion came and instead of eating him up, it stroked and hugged Androcles. It was the same lion that he had helped in the forest! Shocked at this strange behaviour, the emperor demanded an explanation. When Androcles explained what had happened, he was pardoned and freed. The lion was let loose to his native forest.

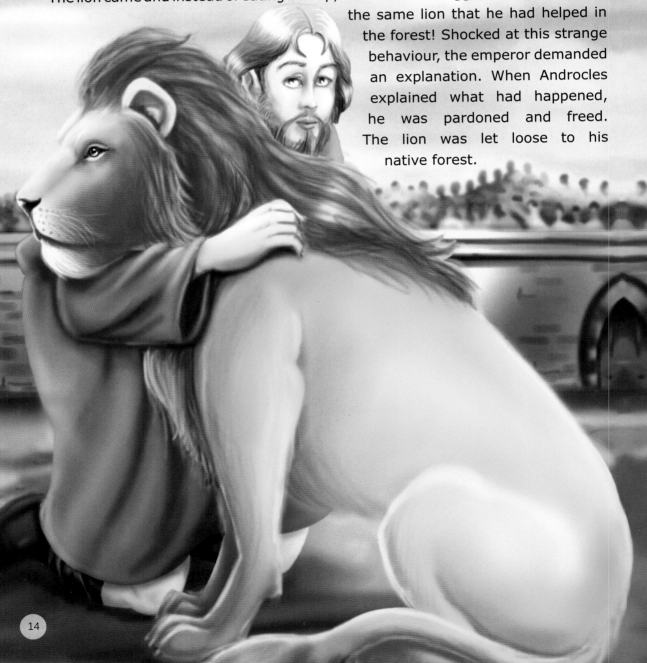

6 The Sparrow Chicks

Once, a sparrow lived in a nest with four chicks. One day, some boys des~~~
their nest, but the little sparrows managed to fly away to safety. The sparrow was
sad that his children were separated from each other and was afraid because the
chicks were gone before he could warn them against the dangers of the world
and the ways to deal with them. After a few months during autumn, when all
the sparrows gathered together for their yearly meeting, he found his chicks in
a wheat field. They were all overjoyed to meet each other and be united again.
The sparrow asked his children how they had spent the summer. The first said
that he had stayed in a garden and eaten caterpillars and worms. The second
informed that he had lived in a royal court, and the third one had spent the
summer on the highway. All the three sparrows had said that they had learnt a
lot about the dangers of the world and how to protect themselves. The fourth
one was the weakest of all the four sparrows. Before he could say anything,
the father asked him to stay with him so that he could protect him against the
eagles and hawks, while his siblings he deemed fit to remain independent. Then
the father asked him where he had spent his summer. The little chick replied
that he had spent his summer in a church and had learnt that he who commits
himself to God need not protect himself for God will be his protector. The father
realised that his fourth son too had learnt everything and would be safe.

7 Waiting for the Train

In earlier times when trains were new, everyone wanted to see a train pass by. Even Old Uncle Theodore, the old lion, wanted to do so. One day, Uncle Theodore heard two birds talking. "The train is coming from the West!" said one. "But I think it will pass only through the desert!" said the other. Uncle Theodore really wanted to see the train chug by. He walked for days in the desert to get a glimpse of the train. For many days he did not drink even a drop of water. The two birds who had seen the old lion waiting, flew to the train and told the engine driver, "Old Uncle Theodore has been waiting for you in the desert for days now! All he wants to do is see your train pass by!" Now everyone loved Old Uncle Theodore. Hearing this, the engine driver fired up the engines. They rushed past the desert in top speed! Old Uncle Theodore was now a very happy old lion.

21 Hunter Rabbit

One day, Hunter Rabbit went hunting. Suddenly, he saw a track of big footprints and thought they belonged to a giant. He found nothing to hunt in the forest and thought that the giant must have hunted everything. Hunter Rabbit returned home empty-handed and ate berries for dinner. The next day, Hunter Rabbit left early but found nothing. He was tired of eating berries. "I must do something," he declared. This time, he decided to lay a net. But the next day, Hunter Rabbit found that a hole had been made in the net. Now, Hunter Rabbit's grandmother was a magician. "I'll make you a magic net that cannot be cut," she said. Next morning, when Hunter Rabbit went to see his net, he saw a blinding light coming from it. Alas! He had captured Mr. Sun! Mr. Sun said, "Let me out, or else, the world will remain dark forever!" Hunter Rabbit quickly freed Mr. Sun. Mr. Sun kicked Hunter Rabbit on his shoulders in anger and his heat turned him brown. That's why rabbits still have brown shoulders and are content with eating berries.

22 The Camel's Hump

Long ago, there lived a very lazy camel in the desert. If ever someone asked him to work, he would snort angrily and say, "Hump!" The other animals would get very annoyed at this. One day, they went to a wizard for help. "Why don't you work?" asked the wizard. "Hump!" grunted the camel. Alas! To his utter amazement, he saw his back puffing up like a mountain. "Here's your hump!" said the wizard. "From now on, you shall work in the desert without food and survive on your hump, because it's full of fat which you can use as food!" said the wizard. Ever since then camels have a hump on their back.

23 Why the Buffalo Walks Slowly

A long time ago, the buffalo and hare were great friends. Both of them used to run very fast. It became very difficult to decide who was the faster of the two. One day, they both decided to have a race and end the argument. The hare started running as fast as he could. But the buffalo ran fast as well and went past the hare. The hare was worried and thought, "If the buffalo runs so fast, he will win the race. I must do something to stop him." So, he went to the buffalo and told him, "My friend slow down, the whole earth is trembling under your weight. I fear if you do not stop running, the earth will sink taking us all under." The buffalo heard this and slowed down and the hare won the race. From that day onwards, the buffalo walks slowly.

24 Jack and the Beanstalk

Once upon a time, there lived a poor widow and her son Jack. One day, Jack's mother told him to sell their only cow. Jack went to the market and on the way he met a man who wanted to buy his cow. Jack asked, "What will you give me in return for my cow?" The man answered, "I will give you five magic beans!" Jack took the magic beans and gave the man the cow. But when he reached home, Jack's mother was very angry. She said, "You fool! He took away your cow and gave you some beans!" She threw the beans out of the window. Jack was very sad and went to sleep without dinner. The next day, when Jack woke up in the morning and looked out of the window, he saw that a huge beanstalk had grown from his magic beans! He climbed up the beanstalk and reached a kingdom in the sky. There lived a giant and his wife. Jack went inside the house and found the giant's wife in the kitchen. Jack said, "Could you please

give me something to eat? I am so hungry!" The kind wife gave him bread and some milk. While he was eating, the giant came home. The giant was very big and looked very fearsome. Jack was so terrified that he hid inside. The giant cried, "Fee-fi-fo-fum, I smell the blood of an Englishman. Be he alive, or be he dead, I'll grind his bones to make my bread!" The wife said, "There is no boy in here!" So, the giant ate his food and then went to his room. He took out his sacks of gold coins, counted them and kept them aside. He then went to sleep. In the night, Jack crept out of his hiding place, took one sack of gold coins and climbed down the beanstalk. At home, he gave the coins to his mother. His mother was overjoyed at their newfound wealth and the family lived happily ever after.

25 Mrs. Littlemouse and the Bumblebee

Mrs. Tittlemouse baked delicious cakes everyday. A bumblebee, who lived nearby longed for the cakes. But Mrs. Tittlemouse disliked insects. If she ever spotted a spider weaving a web, she chased the spider out of her house with her broomstick. "How will I ever get to taste those delicious cakes?" wondered the bumblebee. One day, a butterfly happened to sit on the windowsill. "How dare you come here!" shouted Mrs. Tittlemouse. "Please have pity on me, I have hurt my leg!" pleaded the butterfly. Meanwhile, the bumblebee watched on anxiously from behind a tree. Mrs. Tittlemouse gently applied medicine to the butterfly's wounds and offered some cake. "Great idea!" muttered the bumblebee.

Next morning, the bumblebee buzzed near the window, complaining of a headache. Alas! Mrs. Tittlemouse saw through his plan and chased him away with her duster.

26 How the Alligator Got Its Teeth

About a hundred years ago, there lived in a pond a cruel and greedy alligator. He would hide in the bushes or in the mud and lie in wait for his victim. In those days, alligators did not have any teeth. The alligator used to gobble up whole any living creature that came to drink water in the pond. One day, as the alligator was swallowing another animal, a chipmunk came along to drink water. The alligator got greedy. He thought, "Today I will eat to my fullest. First, I shall eat this animal and then I will eat that chipmunk." Alas! The alligator did not see that the chipmunk was sitting on a thorny bush. As the alligator swam towards the chipmunk with wide open jaws, the chipmunk jumped away and bumped into the thorny bush. All the thorns stuck in his mouth and they hardened to become his teeth. Since then, all alligators have teeth.

36 The King and His Hawk

Once upon a time, a king was crossing a sultry desert. His pet hawk was perched on his shoulder as usual. The hot sun made him thirsty and he went to look for a stream. Luckily, he chanced upon a fountain not very far. He knelt down and was about to drink the water, when suddenly the hawk swooped down and pecked his hand. The king was very surprised at this odd behavior of his pet. He stooped down to drink the water again. But the hawk pecked his hand again. In a fit of rage, the thirsty king drew his sword and killed the hawk. When he stooped down, something glistened in the water. It was a fierce, poisonous snake. The king knew that a single sip of that water would have killed him. He now understood what the hawk had been trying to do. He sat beside the dead hawk and moaned, "I have lost you because of my impatience. All you were trying to do was to save my life!"

37 Piggyback

King Zach ruled the Kingdom of Hackensack. He was so dirty and smelly that no one ever went near him.

"Why do people dislike me?" he asked his minister, Sir Pack.

"That's because you are dirty and stinky," explained Sir Pack.

"What should I do then?" asked the worried King Zach.

"You should scrub yourself well and take a bath," replied Sir Pack.

King Zach rushed to take a bath in the nearby pool. As he emerged from the pool, he said, "Oh! My feet are dirty," sighed King Zach and rushed back to the pool.

When Sir Pack arrived, he explained his problem to him.

"No problem, Master, I will carry on my back but only if you promise to take a bath everyday," said Sir Pack. The king did what Sir Pack asked and no one ran away from him after that.

38 Sylvester and the Magic Pebble

One day, Sylvester, the donkey, spotted a red oval-shaped pebble. He knew that it was a magic pebble that would fulfill his wish. He couldn't wait to show it to his parents. On the way back home, he saw a lion. Fearing that the lion would eat him up, Sylvester made a wish.

"Oh, I wish I was a rock!" The next moment, he became a solid rock. Now, he was safe but how was he going to turn into his old self? The pebble lay close by but unless he touched it, he could never change himself back into a donkey. Sylvester's parents looked everywhere for their son. Tired after the long search, they sat down. Suddenly, his father saw the magic pebble. "What a lovely pebble. Sylvester would have loved it," he sighed and placed it on the rock. Sylvester quickly wished that he could be himself and the next moment, he was back to being a donkey!

39 Sheikh Chilli

Once, there lived a man named Sheikh Chilli. He was a simpleton but was very popular among his friends. One day, the landlord asked Chilli to count the total number of houses in the village. "I will pay you fifty paisa for each house you count!" the landlord said. Sheikh Chilli walked all over the village and counted all the houses and the landlord paid him as per the terms. When Chilli's friends came to know about this deal, they said, "Chilli! Don't you know that the landlord is dishonest? We are sure he must have cheated you!" "Don't worry, friends!" said Sheikh Chilli. "I cheated him this time! I counted hundred houses, but I only told him half the number!" Hearing this, Sheikh Chilli's friends had a hearty laugh.

40 Fool's Luck

One day, a foolish man went to town to sell his ox. He did not tell his elder brothers who were cleverer than him, of his plans. On the way, a sudden storm arose. The foolish man heard the trees creaking and thought that they were speaking to him. He said to the willow tree, "I think you wish to buy my ox." The tree creaked even louder and the fool thought that the tree had agreed to buy his ox. He tied the ox to the tree. He told the tree that he would come to fetch the money later. When he reached home and told his brothers about the deal, they laughed and ridiculed him for his stupidity. The foolish man went back to the tree in anger. He cut down the tree in rage when it didn't give him the money. Lo and behold! He found a pot of gold coins under the fallen tree trunk. The foolish man now became rich but he always remained kind to his brothers.

41 The Good Turn

Gina was the only child of her parents. They doted on her and had thoroughly spoilt her. They fulfilled all her wishes, however unreasonable. Not surprisingly, Gina grew up to be selfish and rude. No wonder the neighbours called her 'The Brat'! Gina's mother had noticed on several occasions that Gina was not willing to share her books or toys with her friends. Moreover, she would bully them and

quarrel with them over little things. Slowly, Gina's friends began to stay away from her. Soon, it was time for Gina to go to school. Even in school, Gina had no friends until Myra joined her class. Myra was a shy and timid girl who didn't mind being bossed around by Gina. She was not a bright pupil. One day, Mrs. Brown the class teacher scolded Myra for leaving mistakes in her work. All the other children laughed at her, making Myra feel miserable. When Gina told her mother about the incident, her mother said, "Gina, you are her friend. You should help her." But Gina shrugged her shoulders and said, "What can I do if she's so dumb?" "That is not a nice way to talk of your friend," scolded her mother. "Let me tell you a story about kindness." Her mother narrated to her the story of an ant and a dove. Once, an ant fell into a stream and was desperately trying to get out of the water. On seeing the ant's plight, a dove who was sitting on a nearby tree, plucked a leaf and threw it close to the ant. The ant quickly climbed on to the leaf and floated safely to the bank. A few days later, a bird catcher was passing by. Seeing the dove he tried to throw a net over it. But the ant saw the bird catcher. Remembering the dove's kindness, the ant crawled up the bird catcher's arm and nipped him sharply. The bird catcher yelled in pain. This alerted the dove who flew away to safety. "So Gina, did you learn something from the story? If you are good to others, then they too will be good to you." Gina listened to her mother's words silently. The next day in class she helped Myra with her work. Mrs. Brown was pleased with Myra and praised her in the class. When Myra thanked Gina for her help, Gina's heart was filled with happiness. One day, in a fit of temper, Gina beat up a girl in school. When the matter was reported to the principal, Gina was told to stay back after school. As a punishment she had to clean all the classrooms. Gina was dismayed. She was a proud girl and could not bear this humiliation. The other children giggled at Gina and made fun of her. After school, Gina sat in a corner and sobbed bitterly. She was surprised when she heard Myra's voice.

"Gina, don't cry. I'll stay back with you and help you to clean all the classrooms. Now let's get started." Gina remembered the story of the ant and the dove. Her mother had been right after all. Gina realised how bad she had been to everyone and decided to be a good girl from that day. Gina and Myra became the best of friends.

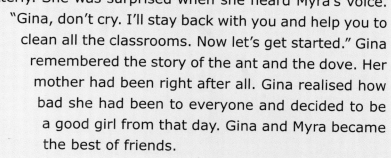

42 The Importance of Hard Work

Tracy was tired of having the bland soup her mother made every day. "I'll not have soup anymore," Tracy said angrily. "I'll serve you better soup in the evening, but for now come and help me dig out potatoes in the garden," replied her mother. Tracy worked with her mother in the garden till sunset and returned home with a sack of potatoes. "Mother, I'm hungry. Please make some soup from these potatoes," said Tracy. This time she loved the soup and took a second helping too. Afterwards, when she asked her mother what special soup this was, her mother replied, "I gave you the same soup I had made in the morning, but you liked it now because you had worked for it the whole afternoon and were tired and hungry after doing so. You now appreciate it more because you realise what has gone into its making."

43 Bill's Reward

Bill was walking back from school one day when he found a black-and-white dog caught in a trap behind a bush. He took the dog home to his parents. "I think it has a broken leg," said Bill's father. "Let's take her to the vet." The vet put a cast on the dog's leg and also told them that she was going to have puppies. Bill was very excited. "Wow!" he said, "I wish she were mine. I must find her owners quickly." He put up signs around the neighbourhood with a description of the dog and his phone number. A few days later, the owner phoned and then came to collect his dog. He praised Bill for taking such good care of his dog. "You are such a good boy that once the puppies are born you may have one for yourself," said the owner. "Oh, thank you," cried Bill overjoyed.

44 Presence of Mind

Gerald lived with his mother and his little sister in a small hut near a railway track. Every day, when his mother would go to fetch vegetables from the market in the evening, Gerald would sit by the window and watch the trains pass by.

One day, when Gerald was babysitting his sister and trying his best to put her to sleep, he looked out of the window and saw that there was a crack in the track. He could hear a train approaching. "I need to stop the train somehow," thought Gerald and rushed out. The train was approaching at great speed. Gerald didn't know what to do. Just then, he had an idea. He took his shirt off and started waving it in the air, frantically. The train driver saw him and sensed that something was wrong. He stopped the train immediately. Everyone praised Gerald for preventing an accident and saving many lives.

45 The Lonely Traffic Light

Tiffany the traffic light, stood at a crossing, blinking red, green and yellow. She was very sad and lonely. "Nobody cares for me!" she sighed. "All they do is drive by so fast!" But Tiffany felt happy when the light was red and the cars had to wait for her to turn green. "Now everyone is looking at me!" she thought happily. Tiffany loved children, who looked out of the car and watched her till she turned green. On some days, they would wave at Tiffany too. One day, poor Tiffany could not change colours. Honk! Honk! All the cars were stuck. Two repairmen came to fix Tiffany. "We need to repair this light very soon! Just look at the traffic jam," they discussed. Now, Tiffany realised how important she was to the cars on the street. "From today onwards, I will work well and keep everyone happy!" She promised to herself.

46 The Three Butterflies

Red, Blue and Yellow were three beautiful butterflies. When they were young, their mother had told them to be loyal to each other. The thick black cloud wanted to put the solidarity of the sisters to test. One day, when they were visiting a garden, he splashed down heavily on their fragile wings. "Let's run to the Gulmohar tree!" said Red. "I will only allow Red to take shelter on my red flowers!" said the Gulmohar tree. "If you do not allow my sisters, I will not stay here," replied Red. Then Yellow suggested that they should rest on the beautiful Amaltas tree. "Only Yellow is allowed here," said the Amaltas. "My sisters are more precious to me," said Yellow angrily. Finally, when the blue Morning Glory also refused, the three butterflies flew away hand in hand. The cloud was happy and cleared away for the sun to shine brightly on them.

47 The Short Tree

A short tree was sad because she could not grow. All the other trees around her were tall and had beautiful visitors like chirpy sparrows and fuzzy squirrels. The short tree longed for a friend. One day, she heard a woodpecker singing in his croaky voice. The tree yelled, "Will you stop singing?" The woodpecker was shocked! "I am a lonely woodpecker and I thought if I entertain people with my songs they would befriend me." The short tree felt sorry, "Will you be my friend?" she asked. "Sure!" said the woodpecker, "But you have to let me stay on your short branch." "And you have to stop singing," said the short tree. The two became great friends and lived happily ever after.

57 The Monkey and the Caps

Once upon a time, there was a young boy who sold caps. One afternoon, while he was taking a nap under the shade of a tree, a group of monkeys came and took all his caps away.

When the boy awoke, he was shocked to see that the monkeys were swinging from the trees, wearing his colourful caps. "Give back my caps!" he shouted angrily. But the monkeys were too busy eating bananas.

So, he thought of a plan. He clapped his hands and jiggled his waist. Since monkeys love to mimic others, they too started clapping and jiggling their waists. The boy then took off his cap and threw it on the ground. The foolish monkeys copied his action and threw their caps on the ground too. The boy quickly collected his caps and left.

58 Going to School

Hooty the Owl was puzzled as none of her students had come to school that day. Only Wily the Turtle had reached school. He liked going to school and learning new things. The other animals had decided to miss school that day and go on a picnic. "I hate going to school to study," said Jumpy the Monkey. "It's so boring," added Croaky the Frog. They were so busy talking that they forgot it was time to go home. Then, they saw Wily returning from school. "Here comes the learned one," said Chirpy the Sparrow, making fun of Wily. The others laughed loudly. Wily told them that he had learnt many new things at school that day. "Do you know the shape of the earth?" None of the other animals knew the answer. "It's round like an orange," replied Wily. "And tell me, what comes first, thunder or lightning?" Again the other animals were silent. "Lightning," replied Wily. They were now beginning to feel foolish and ashamed while Wily seemed wise. "I don't think it's such a good idea to miss school anymore," said Croaky. "Hurrah for school!" added Jumpy.

59 Why Hippopotamuses Live in Water

Many years ago, there lived a hippopotamus called Isantim. Strangely, though everyone knew the hippo, no one except his seven wives knew his name.

One day, the hippo invited all the animals to a feast. Just as the animals were about to eat, he said, "None of you here know my name. If you cannot tell my name, then you all will go back without dinner." All the animals looked at each other.

As no one knew the hippo's name, all of them had to leave without food. "That is unfair," declared the lion angrily. "If anyone can find my name in seven days' time, then I will leave this land forever!" said the hippo. One day, the hippo and his wives went to bathe in the lake. The tortoise happened to be close behind. One of the wives fell down. "Oh Isantim, help!" she cried. When the tortoise came to know the hippo's name, he ran to inform the other animals. The hippos had to leave the land, and have been living in water ever since.

60 Simon and His Old Shoes

Old Simon loved his brown shoes. They were more than twenty years old. He found them so comfortable that he didn't want to give them away and buy a new pair. "Why do I need new shoes? These are better than the best!" he always said. He would wear them for special occasions too. One day, Simon received an invitation from an old friend. Simon took out his old pair of shoes and what did he see! A bird had made a nest in one of the shoes and there lay four little baby birds, sleeping peacefully. Simon frowned and looked at the birds. They were so very small and looked adorable. Simon felt sorry for them. He did not want to make them homeless. So he went to the market and bought a new pair of shoes.

61 Frank and the Fairy

Frank was the son of a poor village carpenter. Everyday, Frank went with his father to the forest to cut trees. One day, tired after a long day at work, Frank sat down on a log to take some rest. Suddenly, he heard a cry, "Help me, please…" He stood up with a jerk and looked about, but there was no one there! "Please help!" Frank heard the voice again. This time Frank peeped into the hole in the log and saw a tiny fairy inside. Frank at once put his hand inside the hole and picked up the fairy.

The fairy thanked Frank saying, "Many years ago, a wicked witch had cursed me and since then, I have been trapped in this log. Thank you for saving me. What can I do for you?" she asked. Frank composed himself and said, "Please make my father rich." "Boommm! Roommm! Zoommm!" said the fairy waving her wand, and suddenly disappeared. "Where did you go, fairy?" cried Frank anxiously. But alas, the fairy had left! That evening when Frank and his father returned home, there stood a palatial house with big iron gates instead of their thatched hut.

They walked in through the gates and were greeted like kings by many servants. Suddenly Frank's mother came running and hugged them and said, "God has answered our prayers." Frank looked up at the sky and imagined the fairy to be among the sparkling stars. He closed his eyes and said, "Thank you dear fairy!"

75 The Wise Judge

Once upon a time, the people of a village decided to hold a ceremony to judge who had the best child. A judge was voted and given the task of choosing the right candidate. The parents with the best looking child would be rewarded. So, one by one, all the parents entered the hall with their children. A merchant who had come with his two baby boys said to the goldsmith excitedly, "Just you see! My babies will surely win this contest. They really are adorable." "Well, you should wait and watch," said the goldsmith who was holding his beautiful daughter. Everyone lovingly spoke of their children's qualities to each other and waited for the competition to start. When the judge came on the stage and saw the proud parents waiting for his decision, he smiled and said, "For all parents, their children are the most beautiful and the best. So how do you expect me to choose one and declare him or her the winner." Everyone clapped at this and cheered for the wise judge.

76 Aladdin

There once lived a poor widow and her son, Aladdin. One day, Aladdin's uncle, Mustafa, came to visit them. He said, "Sister, why don't you let Aladdin come and work for me?" They agreed and Mustafa took Aladdin along with him to a desert. As they walked on, they came to a cave. It was full of riches and treasures but Mustafa was afraid to go inside. He wanted Aladdin to go in and get him the treasures instead. "Go inside," commanded Mustafa, "and find me the jewels. You will also find a lamp. Bring it to me." Aladdin went inside and found more riches than he could ever imagine. He found a beautiful ring and wore it on his finger. But before he could come out of the cave, Mustafa said, "Quick! Just hand me all the jewels and the lamp!" Suspicious of his uncle's behaviour, Aladdin refused. Angry at the refusal, his cruel uncle blocked the entrance of the cave and left. Aladdin sat in the dark and cried. Then he saw the old lamp and decided to light it. While cleaning it, he rubbed the lamp and out came a genie! "Master, I shall grant you a wish," he said. Aladdin said, "Take me home!" In seconds, Aladdin was with his mother, counting the gems he had brought from the cave. Aladdin also brought the ring along with him and when he rubbed it, out came another genie! "Master, I shall grant you a wish!" said the genie. "Make us rich and happy!" said Aladdin. And Aladdin and his mother lived happily. One day, Aladdin saw the sultan's daughter and fell in love with her. He went to the palace with gems and asked for her hand in marriage. The sultan agreed to this. After marriage, Aladdin showered the princess with all the riches and gave her a huge palace to live in. Aladdin and the princess lived happily ever after.

77 The Moon Prince

Little Roger loved to watch the silvery moon at night and wondered if he could go to the moon some day. One night, as Roger was watching the sky, a silver ladder descended from the moon and a handsome prince walked down the ladder. Roger couldn't believe his eyes. The prince walked up to him and said, "I'm the Moon Prince. Come, I'll take you to the moon with me." Roger's joy knew no bounds. He quickly climbed up the ladder with the Moon Prince. "Wow! It's so beautiful!" exclaimed Roger when he saw the huge palace where the prince lived. The prince offered him many mouth-watering dishes and Roger sat on a big chair and ate the tastiest food in a silver plate. Around him were lots of sparkling jewels and diamonds. "Now close your eyes and think of home," said the prince. Roger closed his eyes and obeyed the prince and lo! He was back home in his bed after a wonderful journey!

78 Anansi and the Turtle

Anansi, the spider, once baked some delicious yams. Knock! Knock! Anansi heard someone knocking at the door. It was Turtle. "Can I share your meal?" asked Turtle. As was customary in his country, Anansi couldn't refuse a meal to his guest and invited Turtle, though reluctantly. But, as soon as Turtle sat down to eat, Anansi asked him to wash his hands and sent him to the river. When Turtle returned, he found Anansi already eating. As he sat down to have his meal, Anansi again pointed at his dirty hands. But by the time Turtle returned from his second wash, Anansi ate up all the yams. Turtle then invited Anansi to his house at the river bed for a meal. When Anansi went to Turtle's house, he filled his pockets with stones to avoid floating on the surface. At the dining table Turtle asked Anansi to remove his jacket before eating. But as soon as he did, Anansi floated to the surface and was thus deprived of a delicious meal.

79 The Run Away Clock

The alarm clock stood by the bed every day and ticked every minute. The poor clock was feeling sad, "No one hears me tick all day and night! They only hear me when my alarm goes off at eight in the morning!" "That is what you are supposed to do!" said Chester, the dog. "I am bored and tired of just ticking away!" sighed the alarm clock.

The alarm clock looked outside and saw that it was dawn. It was only five in the morning and there were three more hours before his alarm would ring. "I will go out for a small run," thought the clock. He hopped off the shelf and went to the lawn. No sooner had he walked a little, he came face-to-face with a huge brown dog. The animal growled and barked at him and chased the clock down the road. Just then, a newspaper delivery boy almost ran over the clock. The alarm clock had a narrow escape. "Oh! It is just an hour since I left home and I am already wishing that I was home!" sighed the clock.

Just when he crossed the road to go back home, he found a huge machine with a large brush charging towards him. It was the road-cleaning machine. The alarm clock was drenched in icy cold water and scrubbed clean by the brush. "I want to go home!" cried the clock. But there was more to come his way. A man was clearing the garbage cans in the neighbourhood. He saw the alarm clock lying on the floor, picked it up and threw it into a trash can. He thought that the clock was just a piece of junk.

The poor alarm clock managed to get out of the trash can and hopped onto the road. Thankfully, he saw that he was just two houses away from his own home. The alarm clock looked at his hands and almost panicked. "It is ten minutes to eight! I need to rush back home to ring my alarm on time!" he cried and got up to run into his home. Just then, a little kitten saw the clock. She licked the clock's face and purred. Then, the little kitten dragged the clock to her house. "Why! It's Bitty, the Kitty! I am back home!" said the alarm clock happily. "You indeed are!" replied Chester, the China dog.

At precisely eight, the alarm clock gave out his loudest ring, 'Trrrrrrrrrrrriinnnnnnnnnnng'!

The children and their parents woke up with big bright smiles on their faces. "There goes our alarm clock! On time, as always!" said Mother. The alarm clock was happy to be back home!

From that day on, the alarm clock never complained about anything.

80 Why Crows Caw

Many years ago, there was an owl that had a dyeing shop. All the local birds visited the shop to dye themselves. One day, a crow stepped inside the shop, his feathers elegantly styled and asked the owl to dye him in a colour that would set him apart. In those days, crows were white. The owl led the crow to the dyeing room and put him into a bucket of indigo. When he was taken out, the crow's feathers were straightened and he was glossy black. The crow was terribly furious. He was not in a mood to entertain the owl's logic. He shouted so loud that it cracked his voice forever and since then he could only say "Caw! Caw"!

81 Why the Rabbit has a Short Tail

Long ago, when the rabbit used to have a long tail, he would often disturb the fox lashing his long tail. One day, a fox returned home with a basket full of fish. Seeing this, a mischievous rabbit nearby asked, "Brother fox, how did you manage to catch so many fish?" The fox thought this to be the right time to do something about the rabbit's long tail and said, "Oh nothing. All you need to do is sit with your tail immersed in the water overnight and catch as many fish as you want". The rabbit believed him and went fishing the next night. He did exactly what the fox had told him, quite unaware that the fox wanted to get his tail frozen. All night long, the rabbit sat shivering on a log with his tail in the water. In the morning when he tried pulling out his tail, it was frozen. "Help!" cried out the rabbit and an owl passing by pulled him out by his ears. But lo! His ears grew long and the tail came off. Ever since then, rabbits have long ears and short tails.

82 The Wolf-Donkey

Sandy Rabbit hated carrots. Everyday Mama Rabbit scolded him. "Sandy, if you don't eat carrots, your eyesight will become weak." But he never listened to her. Finally, Mama had an idea. She told Dum Dum Donkey, "Can you come to my burrow tonight and howl like a wolf?" Then Mama went to the squirrel and the sparrow. "Please pretend to be frightened when you hear Dum Dum snarl tonight," she told them. In the evening, Sandy hopped out of his burrow. Suddenly, he saw Dum Dum and was surprised to hear him snarl like a wolf. "Run Sandy, it's the big bad wolf," the squirrel and the sparrow screeched. "It's only Dum Dum Donkey," replied Sandy. "Sandy! Your eyesight was weak and now you can't even hear properly. Didn't you hear the wolf? You could have been in so much danger!" said Mama Rabbit. Sandy ate carrots from that day onwards, without any fuss.

83 The Courage to Stand Alone

One little bat could not understand why he and his kind would always remain aloof from the rest of the animals in the forest and fly only at night. His elders told him that this was because they were naturally superior to all the other creatures in the wild and that he should choose to enjoy this privileged position rather than bother his mind with trivial questions. But the little bat was a curious soul and refused to believe the readymade answers he was given. He went out in the forest to secretly observe the other creatures during the day and decide for himself what the truth was.

After a few days of study, all he could see was simply that the other creatures had just the same kinds of feelings, bonds, relationships and families as the bats. What his elders had been telling him and believing themselves for centuries was not true! The little bat went back excitedly to tell the others in his community what he had found out, but, much to his shock, they refused to believe him, preferring their older views instead and calling him a fool to abandon his special status! Though disheartened, the little bat did not give up. He summoned in himself the courage to go to the forest the next morning and befriend his fellow creatures. To his utter joy, he found a warm welcome in the forest, met different kinds of creatures and learnt lots of exciting new things from them. The bat had tears in his eyes. His persistence and courage had paid off.

84 The Brave Tailor

One day, a tailor was sewing some new clothes when a bunch of flies started troubling him. He shooed them away, but they still continued to bother him. The tailor then took a fly swatter and killed seven flies with one swat. "I have killed seven in a single blow!" shouted the tailor. At this very moment, two ladies were standing outside his shop and talking about a fearsome giant. This giant was killing the people of the kingdom and eating them up. When they heard what the tailor said, the ladies thought that he was very brave and that he had killed seven giants in one blow! They ran to the king and told him about the brave tailor. "Bring him to me!" ordered the king. The tailor tried to explain that he had only killed seven flies, but it was all in vain. "Go, kill the giant!" the king ordered the tailor. The poor man had no choice but to obey. The tailor reached the giant's house. The clever tailor had an idea. At night, while the giant was sleeping, he sewed the giant's mouth together! Now the giant could not eat anything. When he woke up, he begged the tailor to undo the stitches on his mouth else he would die of hunger. The tailor agreed to do so on one condition and said, "I will reopen your mouth only if you promise never to eat any more men!" The giant agreed and the tailor undid the stitches. The giant left the kingdom and the tailor got a handsome reward from the king. Everyone lived happily ever after.

85 The Three Little Men in the Woods

Dorothy went to collect strawberries in the forest. On her way, she met three little men in the forest. "We are hungry. Will you share your food?" they asked. Dorothy gave them the bread she was carrying. Impressed by her kindness, the three men gave her a boon each. One said, "You will get prettier every day." The second said, "You will be very rich." "You will marry a king," said the third. Dorothy was very happy. She returned home and told her stepmother what had happened in the forest. The jealous stepmother sent her other daughter, who was beautiful as well, with a loaf of bread to the forest. She too met the three men who asked her for food, but being very selfish, she rudely refused to share it with them. Angry, they all cursed her, saying that she would get ugly, have two horns on her head and die a miserable death. Many years passed by and one day, Dorothy met a king who fell in love with her, took her to his kingdom and married her. The stepmother could not bear this. Little did she know that it was much more important to be a beautiful human being, rather than just look beautiful on the outside.

100 The Honest Woodcutter

There was once a very poor woodcutter. One day while he was cutting a branch, his axe fell into the river. He was very sad. He had no money to buy another axe. He started weeping. The goddess of the river took pity on him and appeared before him. "Do not weep. I will find your axe," she said and came out with a gold axe. "This is not my axe. I am a poor man. How can I have gold axe?" the woodcutter said sadly. The goddess came out with silver axe next and gave it to him. "This is not my axe either," he said. "I had a simple iron axe." The goddess smiled and came out with an iron axe finally. The woodcutter was very happy to get back his axe and could not thank the goddess enough. The goddess said, "I am very happy with your honesty so take the gold and the silver axe as a gift from me." The woodcutter could not believe his luck. His honesty had changed his life forever.

101 Snow White

Once upon a time, there lived a lovely princess with fair skin and blue eyes. She was so fair that she was named Snow White. Her mother died when Snow White was a baby and her father married again. This queen was very pretty but she was also very cruel. The wicked stepmother wanted to be the most beautiful lady in the kingdom and she would often ask her magic mirror, "Mirror! Mirror on the wall! Who is the fairest of them all?" And the magic mirror would say, "You are, Your Majesty!" But one day, the mirror replied, "Snow White is the fairest of them all!" The wicked queen was very angry and jealous of Snow White. She ordered her huntsman to take Snow White to the forest and kill her. "I want you to bring back her heart," she ordered. But when the huntsman reached the forest with Snow White, he took pity on her and set her free. He killed a deer and took its heart to the wicked queen and told her that he had killed Snow White. Snow White wandered in the forest all night, crying. When it was daylight, she came to a tiny cottage and went inside. There was nobody there, but she found seven plates on the table and seven tiny beds in the bedroom. She cooked a wonderful meal and cleaned the house and, being very tired after all the work, finally slept on one of the tiny beds. At night, the seven dwarfs who lived in the cottage came home and found Snow White sleeping. When she woke up and told them her story, the seven dwarfs asked her to stay with them. The dwarfs loved her and cared for her. Every morning, when they left the house, they instructed her never to open the door to strangers. Meanwhile, in the palace, the wicked queen asked, "Mirror! Mirror on the wall! Who is the fairest of them all?" The mirror replied,

"Snow White is the fairest of them all! She lives with the seven dwarfs in the woods!" The wicked stepmother was furious. She was actually a witch and knew how to make magic potions. She now made a poisonous potion and dipped a shiny red apple into it. Then she disguised herself as an old peasant woman and went to the woods with the apple. She knocked on the cottage door and said, "Pretty little child! Let me in! Look what I have for you!" Snow White said, "I am so sorry, old lady, I cannot let you in! The seven dwarfs have told me not to talk to strangers!" But then, Snow White saw the shiny red apple, and opened the door. The wicked witch offered her the apple and when she took a bite poor Snow White fell into a deep sleep. The wicked stepmother went back to the palace and asked the mirror, "Mirror! Mirror on the wall! Who is the fairest of them all?" The mirror replied, "You are, Your Majesty!" and she was very happy. When the seven dwarfs came home to find Snow White lying on the floor, they were very upset. They cried all night and then built a glass coffin for Snow White. They kept the coffin in front of the cottage. Prince Charming, going past the cottage, saw Snow White lying in the coffin. "My! My! She is so beautiful! I would like to kiss her!" he said and he did. Immediately, Snow White opened her eyes. She was alive again! The prince and the seven dwarfs were very happy. Prince Charming married Snow White and took her to his palace and lived happily ever after.

OTHER TITLES
IN THIS SERIES

978-93-81607-39-8

978-93-80070-77-3

978-93-81607-35-0

978-93-80069-57-9

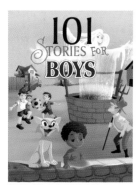

978-93-80070-75-9

978-93-80069-90-6

978-93-80069-85-2

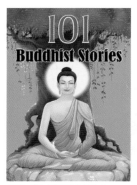

978-93-80069-58-6

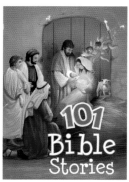

978-93-80069-87-6

978-93-80070-76-6

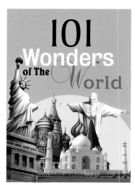

978-93-80070-78-0